For God, who gave me such a delightful character to write about; my friend Natalie Provenzano-Brodie and my husband, Desmond Finbarr Nolan, who both listened to Mrs. McGee's escapades until their ears burned; and for my dad, Alvin, who opened up dozens of coconuts lickety-split for me when I was a kid – A.Z.N.

For Gill – P.C.

tiger tales

an imprint of ME Media, LLC
202 Old Ridgefield Road, Wilton, CT 06897
First U.S. edition 2009
Text copyright © 2009 Allia Zobel Nolan
Illustrations copyright © 2009 Peter Cottrill
CIP data is available
Hardcover ISBN-13: 978-1-58925-079-6
Hardcover ISBN-10: 1-58925-079-6
Paperback ISBN-13: 978-1-58925-414-5
Paperback ISBN-10: 1-58925-414-7
Printed in China

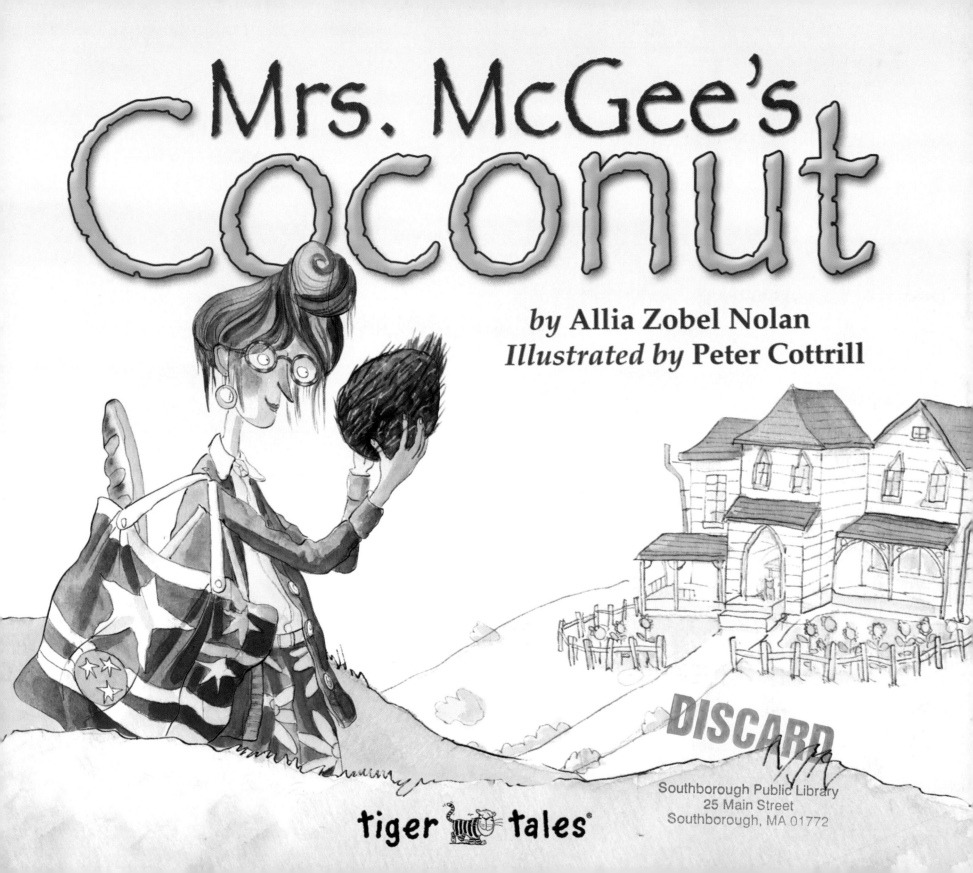

Mrs. McGee's Coconut

by Allia Zobel Nolan

Illustrated by Peter Cottrill

tiger tales

There once was a lady named Mrs. McGee,
who purchased a coconut in Tennessee.
"I'll open it for you," the grocery man said.
"No, thanks," said the Mrs. "I'll do it instead."

"Come look!" said the cat to her good friend, the mouse,
when Mrs. McGee had returned to the house.
The Mrs. was **WHACKING** something on the floor.
She **TH-WHACKED** it so hard that it . . .

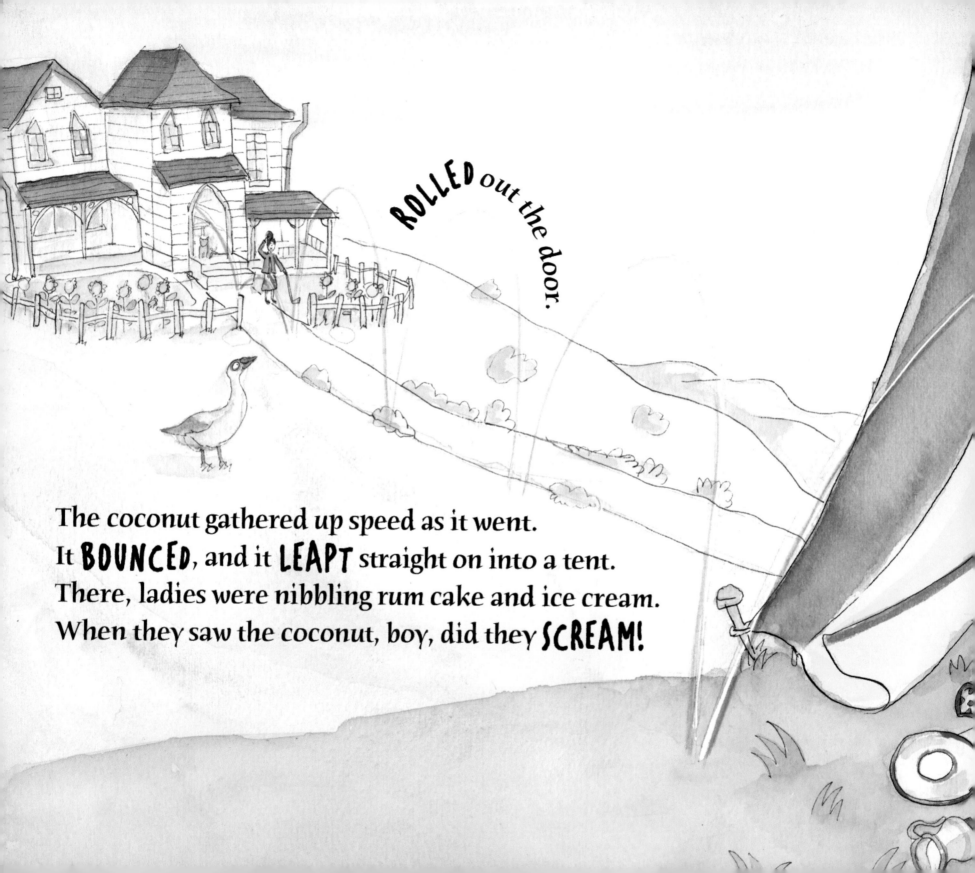

ROLLED out the door.

The coconut gathered up speed as it went.
It **BOUNCED**, and it **LEAPT** straight on into a tent.
There, ladies were nibbling rum cake and ice cream.
When they saw the coconut, boy, did they **SCREAM!**

They jumped from their seats, and they ran outside fast.
They peered at this hairy thing as it flew past.
The coconut flattened a cat named O'Mally,
then **THUNDERED** on into . . .

the town's bowling alley.

It spun down a lane, hitting pins for a ... STRIKE! ... then sailed out the door ...

onto a motorbike.

Of course, it was driven by Mrs. McGee.
When she saw the coconut, she yelled, **"YIPPEEEE!"**
But on the way home, she hit bumps in the road.
You guessed it. . . .

The Mrs. lost her precious load.

The coconut **RACED** down a hill toward a tree;
waiting there with a shovel, stood Mrs. McGee.
She swung at the coconut as it whirled by.
But she missed, and then let out . . .

a TERRIBLE cry.

ARRRGH!

A black-and-white dog chased it down to the pier.
It **DROPPED** in a ship . . .

on its way to KASHMIR.

The coconut **BOUNDED** from ship to the shore
on an island with lizards and parrots galore.

A smart monkey grabbed it.
And wouldn't you know?
He climbed up a tree and then . . .

The coconut opened and, wow, what a treat!
The animals gathered and had some to eat.

Meanwhile ... Mrs. McGee bought some walnuts, and well ...

Now, that is a **WHOLE** other story to tell.